James Greig Smith

**Woodspring**

James Greig Smith

**Woodspring**

ISBN/EAN: 9783337365455

Printed in Europe, USA, Canada, Australia, Japan

Cover: Foto ©Andreas Hilbeck / pixelio.de

More available books at **www.hansebooks.com**

# WOODSPRING

BY

JAMES GREIG SMITH

Printed for private circulation

BRISTOL

J. W. ARROWSMITH, QUAY STREET

1898

# CONTENTS.

# Introduction.

# James Greig Smith.

**A**MONG the small bequests left by a man whose life's work is a permanent legacy to his fellow creatures are found a collection of short essays and sketches on subjects far removed from those by which his name is known and honoured. They are light-hearted sketches in praise of golf, in description of the Woodspring Golf Club, and in affectionate caricature of some of its members—pictures in which he has neither spared himself nor failed to find amusement in his own weak points.

To us, the members of the Woodspring Golf Club, who have lost in him our most enthusiastic if not our greatest golfer, our

2

most appreciative if not our least dogmatic critic, and one of our most valued comrades, these essays have naturally a peculiar interest; but it also seems to us that, inasmuch as they show a side of Greig Smith's character probably unfamiliar to many of his friends, and may give a peep of his spirit at play to those who have only been accustomed to meet him when there was serious work on hand— for this reason alone they are worth preserving in printed form, for private circulation amongst those who valued him.

It is certain too that this course would have pleased himself. In these scraps of literature, written in odd half-hours, for recreation after a hard day, or on a railway journey after an operation, he took a curious pride. He read them to us with an almost boyish delight, and it was his intention to add considerably to what he had written. He even proposed that

other members should add contributions and
that the collected papers should be published.
Brief, therefore, as they are, it has been decided
to preserve them, less for their own sake than
on account of their value as mnemonics; for
their turns of thought, or tricks of phrase
which may help to bring back a vivid picture
of the writer, or awaken memories of his unfailing readiness in good talk—welcome, in
spite of protest, even when it was instructive,
nothing less than delightful when it was not
serious.

He was the discoverer of the Woodspring
Golf Links, and never failed to show something of the pride of the pioneer in speaking
of them. The date of his discovery is uncer-
tain, but the member whom he speaks of as
"the Author" well remembers a Sunday of
uncompromising rain, some three winters ago,
when he was compelled to go with him to spy

out this promised land with an eye to sub-
sequent possession. The ground was muddy,
the lies looked indifferent, the rain blotted out
the views; but there was a finely diversified
course, undoubted possibilities, and nothing
could damp the enthusiasm of the guide. He
laid out a course in his mind's eye, played
imaginary strokes, expounded a new theory
on the art of driving, selected a spot for a
club house, and, with the water running down
his neck, surveyed in fancy from its verandah
a sunset over the hills of Wales. The Author
was not sufficiently appreciative to please him,
which caused him to remark, " It needs a poet
to understand the charm of the place ; " and his
companion, while perceiving the rebuke, was
too uncomfortable to reply.

After this it became a custom with Greig
Smith to take men occasionally to see the
place. He appeared, like the Ancient Mariner,

to know his man instinctively—he fixed him with a glittering eye and told his story. And thus the Man-of-No-Possessions, the Epicure, and others, were numbered among the believers. Ultimately the "octave" referred to in his preliminary essay was complete. The ground was taken in hand, and, aided by the moral and legal support of some and the agricultural genius of one of the fraternity, he had the satisfaction of seeing his dream fulfilled in the creation of a golf links where excellence of course and charm of scenery were combined.

Here, week by week, it became our custom to meet, and it was a rare occasion when Greig Smith was not among us. Something of the seclusion—something, perhaps, of the old spirit of comradeship—of the Priory still remained about the place, and in it he found a rest and refreshment after Herculean labours.

No man of his age had had more constantly
to face and fight for others against death.
He lived in an atmosphere of danger : the
strain and excitement of critical operations,
severe even when they ended in victory, almost
unbearable when they ended in vain, could not
fail to tell upon him, to make him look and
generally to seem older than his age; but here
among his golf clubs, years seemed to be
lifted from his head.   His spirits never failed—
whether he was using his niblick in a bunker, or
sunning himself in the garden after lunch and
explaining why he had failed to "down" the
Sportsman, his great opponent, that morning,
or in the evening at dinner, and long after
it, when there were "few subjects he left
untouched, and none that he did not adorn,"
—at all times here he was alert and stimulating.

The tendency to talk out of season, excellent
though the talk was, was one of those weak

points which the essays show he perceived
himself and which his companions were not
slow to make him understand.   Keen golfer
though he was, he seemed to have a heart
which owned but a half allegiance to the ball.
The other half was always with the scenery,—
with the sunlight on the distant hills, the
shadows on the waters of the Channel, the
passing ships, or the flight of barrow ducks
on the moor; and of these things he would
sometimes speak incontinently when such a
fierce comrade as the Man-of-No-Possessions
was about to make one of those rare strokes
for which he is celebrated.   The result was
not without advantage, and before long Greig
Smith (the Professor as he dubs himself) ceased
to commend the landscape or offer suggestions
for the remodelling of the whole course, with
a ball waiting, teed up.   The chaff he got
on these little points he took admirably, and

showed his sense of humour in never failing to appreciate a joke against himself. At other times his brilliant conversational power was welcome. Even at its worst, that was when it was charged with valuable information and abounded with facts whose accuracy no one else present was in a position to dispute, it was very admirable. There was a conspiracy to prevent him from imparting information; knowledge, in the opinion of one member, was the sworn foe of conversation :—if once the facts were known, there was nothing more to be said; and perhaps amongst the majority of us there was an honest dislike to knowledge. The Sportsman seconded by the Soldier were in the front of the combination, and generally succeeded in restoring the balance of ignorance.

And there was another combination in which we all joined against him. Secretly we might admire the Scottish character, revel in the scenery of Scotland; but so confident was Greig Smith of the superiority of all things north of the Tweed, that we would admit no excellence that was not found south of that stream. He had a fine taste in literature, but his zeal for Scotland led him into some errors of judgment—or rather errors of defence, for it is probable he argued against his conviction. Such was his defence of the Kailyard School of writers, about whom he and the Author had nightly disputes, the commencement of which was the signal for the Epicure to go to bed; for the Epicure is an eclectic in his literature as he is exclusive in other things, and the Kailyard had for him no existence.

The Author was also rash enough at times to discuss the merits of Burns with him, generally getting the worst of it and losing more than one bet on a question of text. But once he triumphed, once he was right in saying that Burns used the word "gae" where the Professor said it was "gang." Though corrected, he was not overcome; his reply was characteristic. "Tell it not," he wrote, "at Sand Bay, whisper it not on the links of Woodspring, but Burns's Scotch was *not always what it should be;* but perfect poetry and perfect Scotch would be impossible in one man, and had he been a 'man of the Mearns' like myself he would have written 'gang,' not 'gae.'"

Such was the man : he defended every inch of ground, he never gave way, but he saw the humour of his own attitude and secretly laughed at his own obstinacy.

In argument he delighted. Constantly in the evening he had the whole room arrayed against him, but he was always ready to play against the best of two—or any number of balls, to borrow an illustration from his favourite game. Nor did we hesitate to take any advantage that offered; for, to continue the illustration, he was often interrupted when about to play his own stroke, and often, as it were, found his ball buried by the innocent foot of the Sportsman.

They were merry evenings, pleasant to look back upon, and very largely dependent for their spirit on the vitality of this lost comrade. No one can fill his place: no such theorist remains to set right our game of golf, no such enthusiast to glorify our links; nor at the dinner table, nor in the smoke-room, nor at bedtime when there should be punch to brew, shall another be found like unto him.

His companions at Woodspring had a good opportunity of seeing how keen a student he was of Nature. He was always observing and always recording some new thing; one of the last problems which occupied him being

the quality of the turf on anthills, and the
comparative absence on them of flat blades
of grass. And if he was not occupied with
Nature, it would be with human nature.
Character was an unfailing source of interest
to him : the man of science came out in
his careful and accurate observation of small
characteristics,—the artist in the use he made
of his material, his firmness of touch in the
sketch or portrait. Indeed, there was nothing
more noteworthy about the man than the
variety of his interests, his wakefulness of
mind — an alertness which gave us an im-
pression that he was living, intellectually, faster
than other men. So, undoubtedly, he was;
and at Woodspring, probably, he found it
easier than elsewhere to drop into a leisurely
pace. Everything favoured it—the peaceful-
ness of old crumbling masonry, the benediction
of sunshine on garden-walls four hundred years

old, were here; and truly after a good morning's golf, and with the solace of tobacco, few better places could be found wherein to forget Time's order to "move on."

Greig Smith loved every inch of the place: the old priory buildings turned into a farm-house, the beautiful tythe barn, the old gate-way with the shields, and the farmyard itself with the familiar sounds that seemed rather a part of the reposefulness of the place than an intrusion on it; and the talk of the rooks in the trees beyond the farmyard, and the knowledge that the world was far away and that there was not so much even as a decent road to lead you back to it—all this had its soothing influence upon his attractive mind. More than his companions did he feel the attractiveness of the scene, for, more than they, did he need rest. His companions here did not know him in harness. They can believe that those who saw him at his labours, who beheld his genius and his courage, may have looked on him as something of a hero, seen in him—

> " Another Hercules
> Battling with custom, prejudice, disease."

To his Woodspring friends this side of him was little known: for us he was the enthusiastic golfer, the witty companion and the kind friend. This is the memory we treasure, and a happier memory will not often be found.

# Of the Club Generally.

# Of the Club Generally.

THE Woodspring Golf Course is one of
the longest in England, and the Club
is perhaps the smallest. It consists
of only eight members, and any addition to
the number is barred. As in other clubs there
is an annual subscription, but the amount of
this under the management of the present
Secretary is unknown.

The old Priory of Woodspring was founded
for ten canons of the order of St. Augustine;
we are two less in number, but, like our
brothers of the older foundation, we seek
seclusion from the world, keep before us a
standard of excellence, and are not indifferent
to our comforts. Each of our octave of golfing

4

canons is known by an adoptive name; he
may have possessed in former times a worldly
appellation, he may still be remembered in his
own country as Mr. Somebody, but here he
receives no such distinction. We know them
as follows: the Prior, the Epicure, the Professor, the Author, the Sportsman, the Soldier,
the Minor Canon, and the Man-of-no-Possessions. They are all excellent golfers, and
whatever they lack in execution they make up
for in the super-excellence of their knowledge
of the game. They are critics of golf, charitable critics of each other's game, desiring less
to "down" than to improve one another, but
inclined to go their own ways in spite of mutual
counsel, and to disregard the theoretical in-
struction which the Professor is always ready
to impart.

The Professor has some knowledge of the
anatomy of the human frame, which he has

brought to bear upon the golf-swing; and in the hope of improving the game of the Club, he reduced certain axioms to writing, and illustrated them with pen-and-ink sketches. They were not seriously received. The Sportsman, whom he had specially in view, craftily changed the subject whenever it arose, and the Soldier remained unimpressed. One or two passages may be given as examples of the pearls of golfing wisdom thus treated. "It is impossible," read the Professor, "to rotate the pelvis on the hips, as Egerton says, when the pelvis sweeps round the thighs; the thighs must follow, because the thighs cannot be straightened beyond the perpendicular." Quoting this with an eye on the Sportsman, the latter appeared not to have heard, and asked the company generally whether it is considered good to do the fifth hole in four. The Professor, with an eye now riveted on the Soldier, again observed:

"The hips cannot rotate round a vertical axis
at all; the left hip can swing round the right as
a centre if the left knee is bent." Whereupon
the Soldier offered to play the Professor for a
consideration, and give him a stroke a hole.

But our Club does not live for golf alone. It
has a pretty taste in vegetables, it knows something about mutton, and is not ignorant of
vintages. The Epicure has an infallible judgment in wine which he permits us to test; the
Soldier's champagne is not without its admirers;
the Sportsman brings out odd lots of good
sorts which we find it pleasant to taste and
criticise, and the Man-of-No-Possessions appears
to have laid up or rather laid down for himself
some treasure in brands. Our property in wine
on evenings after golf is common, at least as to
all of us except the Author, whose cellar seems
limited and who is apt to forget; but even he
occasionally produces a quaint bottle of claret

which is not unworthy. We know something too about music; most of us sing, and sing well. Some are permitted to play the piano, but the Soldier and the Sportsman meet with least opposition when they essay. The Author is believed to have written a song about golf, and we allow him to meander through strange harmonies for awhile in the hope that the song will come, but we have not yet heard it. The Epicure is the only person who is positively forbidden either to sing or play.

Five of us are bachelors, and therefore we think we know something about women. The three married men smile as they hear the Club talk, but they do not interfère; and, though perhaps the knowledge displayed resembles the Professor's golf theories, which, in spite of their excellence, are difficult to carry into practice, it must be admitted that here, in seclusion from the disturbing element, we, like the old canons, may discuss the subject without danger, no distant disturbing petticoat upon the green, no mixed foursomes to mar the tranquillity of our Sabbath day.

We have rules in our Club, but not many. The member who, during a meal, mentions a single stroke of his own by way of boasting, is subject to a fine. Though the number of members is limited, there is no restriction as to the number of friends they may introduce as visitors. A member is damned not so much for himself as for the friends he may bring; the member himself we know and can kick, and do kick, but his friends we cannot, though once or twice we have desired to do so—not often, however. Again, a man who takes medicine has two strokes deducted from his handicap for every dose he takes the day before a match : we want our members to be natural players, and frown on all artificial aids to success. Also we want to keep them healthy. A fine should be added to prevent members from excusing bad play under the shelter of indisposition.

It has been said that no match was ever yet lost by a man in perfect health, and some of our strategists prepare themselves for possible defeat by preliminary hints as to the state of their stomachs. On the morning before the great match between the **Professor** and the Man-of-No-Possessions we were not surprised to see the former limping in to breakfast and cautiously lowering his body into a chair, groaning with rheumatism, while the latter crawled in and said he was an utter wreck and loathed the idea of breakfast. When they began to gird themselves up for the fray, the Man-of-No-Possessions ostentatiously put an elastic bandage round his left knee, stopping now and then to rub his right shoulder. He said that it was acutely painful,

and he had rubbed it with some horse liniment
that morning, and it certainly smelt as if he
had. The Professor put on his vermilion belt
and tightened it to the utmost, swallowed a
teaspoonful of salicine in water, and sat down
on the floor with his back close to the fire,
pathetically asking whether he were to be
driven or carried to the first tee. But at lunch
time it was not difficult to detect the winner.
The Professor cheerily swung into his place and
sat down without a groan, while the Man-of-No-
Possessions limped more than ever, and was
gravely apprehensive that he was lamed for
life.

Then there is the case of the Epicure, who
gets headaches from the excessive freshness and
vigour of the air. For this he takes, the last
thing at night, a mysterious medicine prescribed
by his distinguished physician. When it fails
play is hopeless, when it succeeds—well, he

never knows till the match is over which it will do. Then we all know.

The Minor Canon suffers in some mysterious way in his stomach. For this he stays in bed and treats himself with hot mustard-poultices and total exclusion of light. To us, anxiously enquiring, his brother gives answer that it is nothing; but it is enough to damage the play of the Minor Canon for weeks.

The Author and the Sportsman are never ill. We wished to be sure, and made the Author drink his own wine one night, but it was no use; though he looked jaded the next day, he would not admit indisposition, and his play was worse than ever. The Sportsman once smoked a cigar, given to him by the Man-of-No-Possessions; he stayed in bed all the next day, so we never knew the effect on his play.

The Soldier gets golfer's back and golfer's wrist, and wears a belt for the former and a

5

bracelet for the latter; but as he holds the record of the links, there is rarely any necessity for his being ill.

Week by week we meet together, and pass here some of the pleasantest days and evenings of our lives; and if we cannot claim all the virtues of the original canons, we have at least their bond of fellowship and share their love of seclusion from the world. We have, like them, a Prior, one who has all the qualities a Prior should possess, and the only fault we can find with him is, that other spiritual duties in the diocese take him from us on many a Sunday when we would gladly have him in our midst. His discipline is lenient, his rule benign, and we will not irreverently criticise his game of golf; but of the rest of the brotherhood, the seven canons, we have now some truths to tell.

# The Man=of=No=Possessions.

# The Man-of-No-Possessions.

**H**E does not possess a watch or a pencil, or a silver-mounted dressing-case containing a button-hook. He knows when it is time to get up in the morning by wandering into his neighbours' rooms and asking what the time is. He never has a pencil to mark his card; but he shows you how, by cutting your pencil into two, he can make one for himself. He has the worst legs and the best leggings in the Club; but, as he is dependent on his groom's hands and his groom's button-hook for putting them together, he wears the leggings only on Saturday and is without them on Sunday.

He has a fine fatherly way with caddies, and

teaches them well. Sometimes he awes or even frightens them. One dear little fair-haired caddy he one day terrified, so that he threw down his clubs and ran home screaming. "He was a-scolding of me," the child explained afterwards, "when something in his mouth cracked and broke; and he spit it into his handkerchief and put it into his pocket, and then he talked *orful*, and I was terrible feared and ran away." The Man-of-No-Possessions has a valuable but insecure set of teeth.

He also has nine horses and contrives diabolic devices to make sure that his grooms exercise them, for they are too numerous to be used. He hunts as regularly as rheumatism and the repairing of his numerous injuries permit him to. For indigestion he takes lemon in his tea; but no one yet has discovered the principles on which his boots have been constructed or his breeches fitted.

He is secretary, and keeps the minutes. This he does in the largest hand and the fewest words on record. Resolutions which he considers too long or too wordy, he positively refuses to enter: he has other reasons for excluding other resolutions. As the meetings of the Club are called chiefly for the purpose of rescinding resolutions passed at previous meetings, the habit is not so harmful as it might be expected.

He is also Green Committee. When anything special wants to be done he immediately provides the apparatus; when it wants doing badly he provides twice the apparatus. Thus, when the greens wanted sweeping badly, he sent down six dozen brooms, but forgot to send an army of sweepers. We have plenty of large horse rollers, and he has been for months trying to purchase a donkey.

# The Sportsman.

# The Sportsman.

E has no occupation on earth; and he works harder at this than any amateur golfer. From early morn to dewy eve and well into wet midnight he humbly pursues the fickle goddess of Sport. Sometimes he overtakes her. At golf he recognises the Professor only as his superior. To his own maiden-aunt he admitted this when she congratulated him on always appearing in the paper with the highest score for his round. "Not always," he modestly protested; "the Professor sometimes makes a bigger score, but only the Professor." And the Professor and he play many a round

43

together, chatting and laughing, and boasting and wrangling, and jeering at and praising each other, till the whole Club is scandalised at the levity with which they treat the royal and ancient game. Nevertheless they seem to enjoy it.

The Sportsman does not confine himself to golf. He sneaks off now and again on a yacht; anon he hails from a Scotch salmon river; about the twelfth of August he is on or near to a grouse moor; and on a few occasions he has been seen at race meetings.

He has a fire in his room at nights, and *says* he is always up at five in the morning. His tea, however, is not brought to him till eight. He has a lovely touch on the piano and some ideas on harmony, and no one in the Club can get a good cigar unless he gives it away. It need scarcely be added that he can show a feather for every woodcock he has shot, and that he carries these about in his dressing-bag. Needless to add, they are not few. He is a good shot, is the Sportsman; it is a pity he is so weak in his stockings and gaiters.

# The Epicure.

# The Epicure.

NTIL he purchased the Club donkey, the Epicure bore all the burdens of the Club. The highest form of epicureanism is to give pleasure to others, and we are careful to see that our Epicure has this privilege. We leave undone that which we ought to do, for we know that our Epicure in his impatience will do it for us. When we decided that all members' property should be common property, we had the Epicure in our minds. Who to arrange the sweeps and the handicaps, and to print the cards, and to tip the servants and the cabbies and the gate-openers and the guards, who but the man who bothers about these things—the Epicure?

7

His most triumphant success was certainly the purchase of the Club donkey. Our horsey secretary, the Man-of-No-Possessions, said he had been for months diligently looking out for a donkey to pull the horse rollers. We knew he lied and said so; but the Epicure alone acted upon this knowledge. He certainly bought our donkey; we suspect that he bought several. It was a bargain; for the man he bought it of himself told the Epicure that he had been offered more money for it by two people—one a man from Hampstead, and the other a woman from the Bristol fish market. The Epicure is never without lumps of sugar with which to feed the donkey; naturally we named it Epicurea.

The difficulty about finding a four-wheeled carriage which would convey the Epicure's luggage and the members of the Club from the station was solved when the Epicure decided not to bring down his first dressing-bag. We were sorry for this; for, when we discovered that this dressing-bag was fitted to supply all reasonable wants of a civilised man, and had begun by asking for and finished by taking whatever we wanted, we missed it. It still contained a few trifles when the Epicure decided to bring it down no more. Fortunately his second dressing - case contains many things that we find useful.

We take an interest in the diet of the Epicure. He makes a poor show at breakfast. He tees up an egg and tops it; he gets bunkered in a chop and lifts; he slices on to marmalade and toast for his approach, and holes out always in a cherry-wood pipe with a muddy bottom. His luncheon we eat for him. Prepared at home by his own special cook, brought down and opened and served by his own special servant, we consider it altogether too sumptuous for consistent play if eaten by one man; so we spread it over eight, and find it good average food for golfers. In the way of wines, all that the Epicure has is good. This we know, for we always try it. When he says that '84 Giesler, or '51 port, or '74 Mouton Rothschild are good, we deny it and dare him to prove it : he dares and we drink, and now and then admit that he was right.

What, for a golfer, the Epicure does not possess is not worth possessing. In clubs, balls, boots, gloves, belts, stockings, gaiters, and club cabinets he is up to date. A man invented a club case with a special lock; the Epicure telegraphed for six to be sent to six of the clubs he belonged to. The servant at our Club thought it was a wine bin, and put away the Epicure's liquor in it, and went out playing with the key in his pocket. How the Epicure, coming in thirsty, utilised the legs of his photographic camera to break open that case to get at his liquor, and what he said to the servant when he returned, will be chronicled hereafter.

The Epicure regulates his golf life by gilt things with silver faces like watches, which he keeps in morocco cases. They tell about the heat and the cold, the drought and the moisture, and the height above the sea level, and the pressure of the air and the direction of the wind, and so forth ; and he arranges accordingly. One day his apparatus had made him decide to have his Ross impervious coat waiting at the fourth hole, his medium macintosh cape and petticoat at the seventh, his Scafe boots at the tenth, and his brown gloves at the fourteenth. The weather was two holes ahead of the apparatus, and the Epicure was naturally angry in consequence. The truth was, that the Sportsman had the night before surreptitiously set the apparatus so as to tell him the winner of the Two Thousand.

The Epicure suffers much from the smallness of his hands and the delicacy of his palate. His palms are so tiny that he cannot get a good grip of the Club; so he has to make up for deficiency in breadth of grasp by excessive vigour in gripping—and this hurts.

There is only one thing we will not have the Epicure do for us—that is to sing.

# The Minor Canon.

# The Minor Canon.

THE Minor Canon is always late for everything, and well in the front of everything he is late for, even golf. He is own brother to the Man-of-No-Possessions, and less like him than any other member of the Club. His brother says he hates being ill, and makes a poor show when he is ill; the Minor Canon says the same of his brother. Each tells us in confidence all about the other's illnesses, and we religiously keep their confidences inviolate. How one, bathing, was attacked by some sea beasts and screamed, and how his brother bravely went to his rescue and saved him, would make a good story, but it must not be told.

8

He suffers in some mysterious way in his stomach. For this he stays in bed, and treats himself with hot mustard-poultices and total exclusion of light. To us, anxiously enquiring, his brother gives assurance that it is nothing, and we are beginning to think so also.

The Minor Canon has been on the Veldt, and has lived in waggons and eaten broiled spring-bok. So he lights bonfires on the beach with drift-wood, and we all sit round coughing and wiping the tears from our eyes, and play at camping-out. But we always go in at punch-brewing time, and stay in while the brew lasts,—which means that we never go out again that night.

The Minor Canon drinks his brother's wine and shuns his brother's cigars. He is no fool.

# The Soldier.

# The Soldier.

H E is only a militiaman, but he is a very good one: he might be a real soldier. His experience in the Militia has taught him the wisdom of putting his crest and his initials on everything he possesses—even his golf clubs and his pyjamas.

Now, the Soldier has a fine style of play; he has played much in Scotland, and been coached by Scotch professionals. He makes the ball travel by putting what he calls "beef" into it; so we try to put "beef" into it also. He wears a belt and a red coat, and the very latest fancies in gaiters, leggings, or spats. Some of us try to follow him in these things, and the Professor comes nearest to success.

When the Soldier has won his match and

dined well, he is liable, if awake, to sit down
to the piano and play divinely. He had one
night meandered into some Op. or other which
sounded rhythmic, when a wink passed between
the Man-of-No-Possessions and the Author.
They started to dance a jig, and they danced
well—really well. They skipped, and set, and
crossed, and cracked their fingers, and stuck
out their elbows most beautifully and in
beautiful time, so that the Club sat spell-
bound in silence till it was over, when it burst
into wild applause. The jig was Irish, and
this fired the Professor, who is Scotch. So
he placed the poker and the tongs on the floor,
crossed as two swords, and essayed "Ghillie
Callum." The Professor in evening clothes
weighs fourteen stone; the floor shook, and
the audience was awestruck: it was a fine
performance. But it was a mercy that the
Sportsman, who knows the ways of the Scotch,

was ready with the right restoratives at the finish, otherwise he felt that golf might have been over with him for ever. His golf for weeks afterwards, he admitted, was tinctured with " Ghillie Callum " in his bones. The Club considered that his performance was well worth what he suffered for it.

The Soldier is eminently practical, and shows some contempt for the Professor's dicta on golf. He refused to admit that there was anything in that learned man's theory of the rotation of the pelvis, and said that an ounce of practice was worth a pound of prescription. The Professor therefore sarcastically inquired whether his Rugby education had been sufficiently serious to acquaint him with the composition of the powder he was ready to kill men with.

The Soldier said he did not know and did not care, if it sent the bullet on.

The Professor further wanted to know if it came out of the brain of the British soldier or the German chemist.

The Soldier admitted that it might want a German chemist to invent it ; but only the British soldier could hold the gun straight, and that was the main point after all. So too of golf, this modest fellow added :

" You let the Soldier with his muscles and his clubs loose on the ball, and he will down you and your theories and your diagrams every hour of the day and every day of the week. Good-night ! "

The Author.

# The Author.

WHAT the Author has doubts about he writes about. The only thing he has not written about is golf. He knows golf.

As a man and a golfer, the Author is held in the highest esteem by the Professor; for the Professor has discovered that the Author knows Burns almost as well as he knows him himself, and is constantly boasting of how the Author, a mere Anglo-Irishman, won a bet off him, the Professor, a genuine pure Scotchman, about a certain reading in Burns's poems. First to know Burns, then to know golf : these with the Professor are the first and second steps towards honour and virtue.

For every hole on our links the Author has broken all records—not, it must be admitted, on the same round. His records are in double figures as a rule. But there are exceptions. For instance, he once took on the scratch man of a neighbouring club, receiving a half, and at the ninth hole was eight down. This made him mad, and he challenged the scratch man level for the other nine holes, and beat him three up. The Author never can play till he is exhausted; and as he can always wear out any member of our Club, the inference is obvious.

There is one thing which the Author can do better than any other member of the Club,—and that is, keep his wrists down in his iron approaches. The Soldier says this is rot, but the Professor thinks there may be something in it. He was once beaten by the Author— they have played together only once. The

Author has solved the problem of the grip. For
the left hand, which ought to grip tightly, he
has a mass of india-rubber divided into
segments—a segment for each finger. For
the right hand, which ought to hold loosely,
he has an arrangement set with minute
spikes, so that even in his wildest enthusiasm
he dare not grip hard.

Golf, the Author considers, is ruined by the
weary monotony of play on two or three
links. So last Easter he travelled nine hundred
miles, and in ten days played over eleven links
in Scotland and elsewhere. After playing
three rounds on St. Andrews, he travelled
the rest of the day and all night, and got
on our links weary and unslept and unkempt,
but saturated with the very aroma of the
best game. After the Sportsman and the
Professor (not our best men) successively had
beaten him, he gave a terrible thrashing to

the Soldier (our best man). The Author has seriously considered the advisability of committing some crime which will condemn him to imprisonment with hard labour for six weeks. When released, he feels certain he could play golf as golf should be played. His fellow members discourage the idea, but only, they assure him, for the sake of his wife and family. As a matter of fact, his fellow clubmen are coming to believe that for the Author the royal road to excellence in golf is through either crime or fatal illness. Curiously enough, they would rather that he continued a member of their Club than that he were imprisoned or died.

# The Professor.

# The Professor.

THE only way to keep the Professor quiet was to put him into the chair, so this was done. Here, his behaviour is simply perfect. At most Club meetings his first duty is to reprimand the Secretary for having forgotten to enter any minutes. This he does with great dignity and much kindly feeling.

The Professor would not be described as a good exponent of the practical part of the game, but he is unrivalled in its science and its theory. Most men, when they top a ball, are content to curse and let it pass. Not so the Professor. You top it, he tells you, in the

10

descent of the swing, in the ascent, and at the bottom; and, according to him, the ball either bounds or runs or trickles. If you listen, he will convince you, and then woe betide you! for he will certainly down you. The Professor's humiliation comes on the putting green. He is often further from the hole after a putt than before; he has been known on the twelfth to fail to hole out after the sixth putt, and then to pick up the ball, saying that "jugglery is not a game, it is a question of pure practice."

The Professor makes at least one extraordinary shot in every round he plays, and always tells us of it. On the occasion when he carried on to the green from the tee of the thirteenth, the members were so impressed that the Epicure at once presented him with his untouched luncheon basket, the Soldier with his knife crested and initialled, the Author with his wife's gunmetal watch and leather chain, and the Sportsman silently cast his well-filled purse on to the heap. The drive was worth it : the curious thing is, that he did it. Sometimes he does not.

———

# Some of our Matches.

# Some of our Matches.

## I.

### THE MAN-OF-NO-POSSESSIONS AND THE EPICURE.

THE Man-of-No-Possessions gave a final glance round to make sure that his defeated opponent had gone to bed, and proceeded to describe their round. The Man possesses a clear enunciation and a distinct gift of graphic description, if he possesses nothing else, and his monologues are always impressive even when they are incredible.

" He was at the very top of his game to-day, was the Epicure." This is the way the Man leads us on to asking him to describe his exploits. " I have never seen him play so consistently well."

" How many was he down to you ? " asks the Professor softly, as he rolls another cigarette.

"Three, only three," answers the Man, looking sharply and suspiciously towards the querist.

" Tell us about it," suggests the Author, and we settle down comfortably to listen.

The Man took another vile-smelling cheroot out of his twist of brown paper, lit it, did something to something inside his mouth which fixed something, and proceeded :

" He got the honour at the first tee by tossing a coin. I got it at the second by play. Here I was well on the 'pretty' in my drive, in spite of the gale, but my ball was buried in the hole it made. He with a fine drive was thirty yards behind on the rough, but it was teed up. I had to dig my ball out with my iron, and hurt my shoulder, while he——"

"Did you win the hole?" interpolated the Author.

"No," says the Man.

"Then go on to the next," suggests the Author.

The Man stares, takes the cheroot out of his mouth meditatively, fixes the unstable thing inside, and proceeds:

"I was three down at Ben Barrow. The Epicure never made a mistake. He nearly reached the wall, I carried it."

"Gale blowing behind you?" suggests the Author.

"Not a gale—a breeze, I admit, but not a gale, certainly not a gale. Well, I was level with the green in my second." Here he stopped, took his cigar out of his mouth, and fixed his eye on a member who threatened to smile. Then he resumed: "So I won that hole. I carried the bay. He drove on to the beach, but his ball bounded out on the flat, and he halved the hole, positively halved the hole. It was neck and neck to the thirteenth, he playing a magnificent game, I clinging to him. Well, at the fourteenth I carried everything and lay dead off my drive."

" I've done that myself," interpolates the Minor Canon.

" With the help of a hurricane," admits the Man to his brother.

" Certainly, but not such a hurricane as to-day," insists the Canon.

" Let the Man proceed," the Professor dictates.

" Well, at the fifteenth I drove into the bunker . . . ! "

" *Into the what ?* " screams the Soldier, waking up from what seemed peaceful slumber.

" INTO THE BUNKER," firmly replies the Man.

" WHAT BUNKER ? " persists the Soldier.

"THE FIFTEENTH," repeated the Man-of-No-Possessions.

"Where from?" the Soldier continues.

"Why from the TEE, of course."

There was a death-like silence for a definite number of heart-beats. Then every member emptied his glass, got up and solemnly shook hands with this Man, wished him good-night and went to bed.

## II.

### THE PROFESSOR AND THE SPORTSMAN.

"THAT'S the ball which will make you squirm!" said the Sportsman, as he took his nubbly Agrippa out of the hot-water basin after breakfast and held it under the nose of the Professor. A soft smile spread over the Professor's countenance as he reached out for the Sportsman's wrist, and carefully felt and counted his pulse for a full minute by his watch. He said nothing, but smiled more. The Sportsman did his best to look jaunty, and cordially reminded the Professor of various bunkers which he habitually entered.

The Professor on his good days drives a ball which rebounds backwards about a foot from where it alights. This morning the ground was wet, and it was found embedded in its hole. He was keenly interested in this backward recoil and repeatedly insisted on the Sportsman coming up to see it. Now, when he went over the wall to the fourth green he found the Sportsman on the green close to the flag, and his own ball buried almost out of sight. The Sportsman was most sympathetic and gravely watched his opponent's attempts to dig it out. It cost three strokes. The Professor was having serious doubts as to the excellence of his method of driving, and said that he meant to return to his long slow method, followed by a run. He topped the next, but the change was, he said, in the right direction. Well, at the sixth he found his ball buried from the drive more deeply than ever. He examined it minutely, he saw some-

thing, he gasped, he called up the Sportsman,
he requested him to turn up the sole of his boot.

" Well ? " asked the Professor.

" It *is* well," answered the Sportsman, and
he winked.

" My hole ? " suggested the Professor.

" Your hole," assents the Sportsman, and off
they walked to the next tee arm-in-arm.

" Did you put your foot on my ball at the
fourth also ? " asks the Professor.

" I did," answers the Sportsman.

Thereafter the Professor ceased to take interest
in the burying of the ball and in noting the
cup it made.

As they walked along the ridge to the Pipe
hole they saw the Man-of-No-Possessions labo-
riously arranging himself to putt on the second
green against the Author. They stopped to
watch the proceeding. They caught the eye of
the Man as they stood on the sky-line. This

disarranged him for his putt, and he stood up erect, waved his club and said things. Then the two onlookers called up their caddies and formed an admiring group, and pointed down to the putting green, and shouted back and said they were quite ready and advised the Author to get on with his putting and so forth. Finally when the putting was over and the Man-of-No-Possessions looked as if he meant to charge them, the two walked away, harmoniously condemning the affectation of the golfer who pretends that he cannot play if things take his eye. Nothing could tear their eyes off the ball when they had fixed them on it.

The Man-of-No-Possessions, as Secretary, afterwards called attention formally, at a meeting to this gross breach of golfer's etiquette or rule, and the Professor, as Chairman, had to reprimand both the Sportsman and himself, which he did with much unction.

Later on the two interrupted their match at
the shrimper's hut, and were found eating
shrimps as fast as the shrimp-boiler could
unshell them. They cheerfully let two couples
pass them. This, they were told, put them out
of the competition for the handicap sweep.
After examining their cards they said they
submitted, but they thought it a harsh rule.

At the sixteenth hole they decided that, as
they were out of the sweep and as it was getting
late for luncheon, they would not play the seven-
teenth and eighteenth, and so they finished 'all
square.'

Then at luncheon they talked to each other,
and at the others, in description of the most
marvellous shots they had made in their round.

"What a pity you over-drove the green into
the sea with your second at the Ben Barrow
hole," says the Sportsman.

"What! in his second?" asked a startled

visitor. The members listened without com-
ment.

"Yes, in his second," replied the Sportsman,
helping himself to some more Woodspring
mutton (the best in the world), "and so he lost
the hole."

"Sportsman!" says the Professor, "you must
give up that cleek, it does not give an opponent
a chance. I don't mind your holing a cleek
shot once in a way, as you did at the second.
But to do it four times in one round is too
much."

The stranger ceased eating and drinking, and
stared. The Professor and the Sportsman
unconcernedly went on eating and drinking,
and talked.

## III.

### THE EPICURE AND THE AUTHOR.

ITH the Epicure should have been matched the Stoic; but we have no Stoic in our Club, so the Author, who is full of pluck, took the Epicure on. The two have their points of divergence, however. The Author believes in various things; the Epicure, in nothing save his style of play. How the Author sacrifices to the deity of golf it is our purpose now to describe. The Epicure sacrifices nothing to the Unknown or anything else. The Author may turn up on a Sunday morning, mud-bespattered after a fifteen miles' ride on his bicycle, without balls, clubs, partner, or whisky, and a hungry look in his countenance asking for all four. The Epicure has a threefold set of clubs at every links to which he belongs; his match is arranged days before : he has the largest flask in the Club, and it is never empty; while his luncheon-basket is a poem, and always on the spot at the right moment. The Author never wants while the Epicure has anything; therefore the Author never wants. And this is as it should be.

There was some difficulty about starting these two. The Epicure had gone early to bed, the Author had not. The Epicure never touches spirits at night, the Author always does. The Epicure breakfasted to the minute, the Author was half an hour late. And then, while the Epicure, with his gaiters on for misty (not for rainy—other gaiters for rainy) weather, and his medium thickness suit, without lining on the back of the waistcoat, was walking up and down (not in anger, mind,—he is never angry), the Author was engaged in a hot argument with the Professor as to the correctness of a quotation from Burns. This was, we are sorry to say, left to the settlement of a bet, and we got the two off.

At the first tee the Author explained that he could never play golf till he had done three rounds. If the Epicure cannot play, it is not his fault. He stands right, he swings right, he hits the ball in the right place with the right part of his club; and if the ball does not travel, that is no affair of the Epicure's. So the Epicure walked smiling into the bunker after his ball, while the Author ran cursing down the hill on the right after his. And that was all we saw of them till they turned up on the ninth green after the half-round. Then it was evident that something was wrong.

Here, on the beautiful plateau on which are

spread the velvety ninth and eighteenth greens,
they discovered the Professor and his match,
the Sportsman, breaking all rules of golf by
drinking and reclining in the middle of a
handicap round. To the Professor the Author
went up and asked if he had any golf clubs fit
to use. The Professor said that he had, and
that they were all at the Author's service. The
Author wanted to know whether the Professor
would take a sovereign for a certain iron he
selected. The Professor said he would, and he
did (he is Scotch). Then the Author deliberately
teed up a much-hacked ball, drove it into the
sea with his own iron, broke the shaft of the
club over his knee, and sent the fragments after
the ball. He said nothing, nor did the Epicure,
nor did the others. They went off again, and
were not seen till the last hole. Their drives
were far apart—the Author being away to the
right on the level, and the Epicure to the left

amongst the ruts. He had changed his gloves; they were now a pale yellow, he had started with dark brown ones. Their caddies looked wearied and worried, but each was close to his master's heels.

It was the Author's hole, but he did not seem happy; and when his card, duly added up, was handed to him by the exact Epicure, he first tore it from the top to the bottom, then across, and then in every other direction. He seemed about to cast it to the winds, but changed his mind and put the fragments into his pocket. Later on one of us saw the Author surreptitiously and guiltily slip these fragments into the fire. We never had any further account of the round.

# Lies in Golf.

# Lies in Golf.

E lie a little with discrimination that our guests may lie much with fine art. Of all our guests, the most voluminous and most artistic liar is the Policeman. At first we had to help him by encouragement and by example; but now that he knows the strength of his pinions, he soars off alone on his flights of fancy and lies by the hour unaided. It is real pleasure to listen to him.

Once we had a fat man down, who was no liar at all, but was painfully and minutely precise in his description of his round. On him after dinner we let the Policeman loose.

Not a word would the Policeman utter till the cigar which the Sportsman had given him had

13

burnt its way through his moustache, and was eating its way into his lips. Then he borrowed a pipeful of tobacco from the Professor, lit his pipe, and began.

For ten minutes at least the fat man listened spell-bound. Then we became spell-bound, and did not observe the fat man. On and on the lying went in grave monotone, while we held our breaths in admiring and envious silence.

He had come to the point in his story which described how, being in straits, and finding it necessary to do the Ben Barrow hole (400 yards) in one, he saw a man carrying a bucket full of water to mix mortar for the building going on there, and accordingly drove into the bucket; how he made the man, a living and moving object, move towards the hole, and caused him to pour the ball into the hole.

"And that," complacently remarked the Policeman as he noisily knocked the ashes out of his pipe, "and that is the only occasion on which I have done the Ben Barrow hole in one."

Suddenly upheaved the huge bulk of the fat man. He snorted and stared, and in alarm gasped:

"Did you say *one?*"

"I said 'one,'" gravely answers the Policeman.

"Good gracious! I had no idea it was so late. Good-night all!"

And the fat man shuffled off to bed. Next morning he admitted that he always slept after dinner; but he never remembered having slept continuously till one o'clock in the morning before.

The Policeman is not devoid of courage. He says he would like once again to be let loose on the fat man. We are thinking it over.

# The Woodspring Links.

# The Woodspring Links.

N the following imaginary game we have the Professor's description of the Wood-spring links. Perhaps his fictitious opponent may seem too prodigal in praise of the course, too silent about some of its imperfections. No allusion is made to the superabundance of grass in the early summer, to the rabbits which descend upon the greens in search of buttercup roots and at times give some of them the appearance of bagatelle boards, nor to the worms, nor to the curlews and other enemies we have to contend with. Our Professor loved the place too well to be critical; and if we do not all of us see in it such a perfect golf course as it appeared in his eyes, we are not prevented thereby from sharing in his enthusiasm.

Between Weston-super-Mare and Clevedon, on the south side of the Bristol Channel, a tongue of land juts into the Severn sea, on which an octave of golfers have established themselves and made a glorious links. There are eighteen holes—there might be six-and-thirty—of real good golf, with crisp old seaside turf, such as is found growing on the sandy loam on the Severn shores; and hills and hollows, and slopes and gullies, and whins and rocks, and sand bunkers and a few stone walls. There are no trees or hedgerows, or heather or rushes; but there are most other things. Here monotony does not bore. There are tees on hills to carry valleys; to pitch on levels; and to settle on slopes. There are tees in valleys to carry ridges, and cross gullies, and pitch on plateaux. You may pull or slice into the sea, or down a ridge, or into whins, not to mention a pebbly beach and a sandy marsh. There is special reward for long driving, and special punishment for short. There are holes where a magnificent carry will save two strokes, and where the diligent plodder has not a chance. There is no cramping on this course: a free slashing open game is possible from the first tee to the last hole.

Well, one of the octave—the Professor—asked me down, and I went. He knows a good deal about golf, does the Professor, although he has been at it only a couple of years. The physics and mathematics of the game, the principle of the swing and the follow-through, and the explanation of the carry, and the sclaff and the jerk, and a score of other recondite matters, he has at his finger-ends. And he will be very pleased to give you a few hints on your play,

14

if you will let him,—only don't let him, for if
you do he will down you.

I offered him a stroke a hole, which he
promptly refused. He consented to take a half
after some pressure. So I considered that I, a
scratch player, had a soft thing on. But I
hadn't. And this story of our match shall be
my description of the Woodspring Golf Links.

### I.—THE PRIORY 'HOLE. 280 YARDS.

A fine hole, with a beautiful and cunningly
protected green. A pull gets over a stone wall
out of bounds; a slice lies on a nasty slope.
The Professor warns me that the drive will roll
towards the wall. I ignore him, and it rolls as
he said. Never mind, I pitch it on the green
with my iron, and he follows with his brassie
and runs over on to a road. He gets a
stroke here and halves. Now I look down a

sharp slope on the right, and shudder as I think where I might have been. Sand bunker before the green, admirably placed.

## II.—MIDDLE HOPE. 290 YARDS.

Tee on the edge of a cliff. Here one simply *had* to look around at the view; and the ball, teed for the honour-stroke, had to wait. In front the broad brown Severn sea, and beyond it Penarth Cliff, Cardiff, and the Welsh mountains. To the right the grand sweep of a semi-circular bay, with rich red-brown beach and bright green lining, while the white walls of Clevedon stood out clear and distinct on their hills. Ships are passing up and down, and—"Your honour," hints the Professor.

Another pretty hole—a long strip of flat turf, a raised beach, with the sea on the right; a cliff and sloping turf covered with whins on the left, and the sea beyond the green at the end. One must keep straight here. There is a strongish breeze blowing from the left: I must allow for that. I did: the wind didn't touch it; and I place a long ball on the slope behind a whin-bush.

"Ay, there's a wind up here," says the Professor, "but it's sheltered down there;" and he thereupon plays a decent ball, making practically no allowance for the wind, and getting a beautiful lie. I was cupped, but went for it, dropped into a whin-bush, and had to lift. His hole.

Then a short walk up the side of a cliff, during which the Professor explained to me that even golf wanted brains, and that an idiot might have known that if it blew high up on the tee, it was sheltered in the hollow behind the cliff.

### III.—THE POUND. 250 YARDS.

Tee up on an eminence: carry, a cattle-pen and a pond; slice, into the sea or down a cliff; pull, into a field out of bounds.

His honour; a decent ball, straight and a good lie. Mine better. A sand bunker protecting a pretty and visible hole. I am on the green with my iron; he isn't far off with his brassie. He gets a stroke here, and he halves the hole. One down.

### IV.—SAND BAY. 500 YARDS.

A driving hole, little hazard; uphill; three good drives should lie on the green, the last shot over the wall, a blind approach.

Here, being well over in my third, I had the pleasure of seeing the Professor playing fives up against the wall. I must admit that

he had had bad luck with his third, for he
just topped the wall. A pretty sloping green,
with a ridge in front.

My hole—all square.


### V.—RANGE.   500 YARDS.

Another slogging hole; mostly uphill, with
a dip in the middle. To the left a precipice
waits for the pulled ball. The Professor warned
me of it, and I went down ! I wish he would
let me alone to negotiate hazards I can see.
Of course, I allowed for the wind ; how was I
to know that the wind along the edge of the
precipice went up in the air, and not across
on the flat ? *That* isn't golf ! He began
explaining to me that it was best to go on to
a flat plateau and then go up, and—hang the
fellow !—I went down to show him how to
get up. So I took my lofting iron and hit

a beauty ; it went up and up; pitched on the edge and then came down and down, lower than ever. Another, more slanting,—not up, down again ! I examined my ground. There was the Professor quietly seated on the ridge ; I could see him calmly rolling a cigarette ; I furtively watched him strike a match in the usual place, and the smoke arose in volumes, while he calmly looked on. Six more strokes and I am at the top in a sweating fury.

" That isn't golf," I sneer.

" Then why did you go down there to play golf ? " he mildly asks.

" No man could carry that mountain," I insist.

" Then why did you try to carry it ? There was that lovely lie beyond I told you of. I myself——"

Hang the man ! His hole—one down.

## VI.—SWALLOW TAIL. 230 YARDS.

High tee, over rough ground and a stone wall; bunker on right, tricky sloping green. He got into a bunker on the left.

My hole—all square.

## VII.—BEN BARROW. 480 YARDS.

A fine driving hole. Tee up on the top of the Ben, a small sugar-loaf mountain. Two perfect drives will land you on the green, but the first drive must carry that wall.

" That wall! why it looks 300 yards off ! "

" Never mind what it looks, it isn't 300 yards off, I 've driven it myself," smirks the Professor ; and then he shows how, if you think you can't carry it, you may go to the right opposite that gap in the wall, where there is good lying. To the left, the sea and a hollow threaten ; to the right, a nasty slope. If I can't carry it, indeed!

Well, I went for it, and away the ball soared into the clouds. Will it? Yes!—no!—yes! When will it drop? Over! but only just over! It was an anxious moment. I waited in triumphant calm for his drive. He knew his powers and went for the gap, and rolled into a sort of rut, for which he had to take his mashie and went twenty yards. I get in a stinger, and am informed I must be near the green. He puts in a decent brassie shot, and, with the help of a flukey putt, his stroke halves the hole. Still square.

A fine green on the down slope, with sea on two sides.

### VIII.—THE BAY. 160 YARDS.

Across a pretty bay, with a beach of white pebbles; over some bushes up the face of a steep slope fifty feet high, and on to a pretty green sloping to the drive. It is simply a fair drive, he says: it looks more. And he began to explain that though it is quiet down here on the tee, there is a sharp breeze blowing up there, right in our teeth, and that a low ball which will rise at the end, is better than a high ball which will catch the wind. I drily inform him that I think I understand, and let go. It starts well, rises, then stops, then hovers, then comes back, then rolls down to some path or ridge where it stops.

" We call it sometimes the ' Hole of Sisy-phus,' " he gently remarks, as he takes a short-cut to the right and gets up. " There is less wind there," he remarks. " You see, there is rising ground beyond."

I did not get up in my next, and I lost that hole. One down.

Now we have a walk to the " Pipe Hole,"

as it is called, and a lovely walk it is. The rich Yatton Valley in front, with the Mendips beyond, the Severn and Clevedon on the left, Sand Bay and Worlebury behind and to the right, and the picturesque broken contour of the links, with their little pebbly bays and grey rocks and bright green turf for foreground.

### IX.—PIPE HOLE. 260 YARDS.

A beautiful hole. One perfect drive and one perfect approach lands on the green. Nothing else save luck and miracles will do it. A short drive drops on a sharp slope or a road ; a pull and a top gets into a sort of quarry; a little slice gets into sand bunker or hollow, or somewhere worse. For the approach, two yawning sand bunkers intervene, and a precipice waits beyond. The green itself is as nearly as possible perfect.

Well, I played this hole as a scratch man ought to play it, and did it in four. The Professor took nine, and explained to me in detail why he did so.

All square at the turn. Whisky; and one more look at the glorious views.

### X.—CHANNEL. 230 YARDS.

A level hole, with a perfect green, protected on the left and beyond. Pull, down a precipice or into a valley; top, into a sand bunker.

He warned me of the wind from the right, but I didn't allow enough and got a little way down the ridge on the left. His drive here, I must admit, was a fine one; he was dead with a flukey approach, and did it in three.

His hole—one down.

## XI.—CLEVEDON. 300 YARDS.

The Professor here informed me that he never took more than four over this hole, and always won it. It looked an easy hole, but really wanted playing and judgment,—in the approach especially. He proceeded to explain. I did not listen.

But he got away a good drive, well to the right of the guiding flag. I got a better on to the flag. He hit some sort of a hummock with his mashie approach; I saw the flag and the green and the intervening bunker, and played a careful shot. One ball was on the green, another was over—that other was mine. He certainly did it in four, so did I: but he had a stroke, and won the hole. I confess I was rather sore at his explanation of how he won. I believe I played the hole as it should be played, and the Professor's finessing worried me : " You can't be sure in playing downhill, even a little, that your ball will stop dead unless you pitch on the level or a slope towards you, and in such cases you must put on cut. Now, at St. Andrews, or Hoylake, or Westward Ho ! where I believe you have played, there are no approach slopes like this. Here you must——" and so forth, and so forth. His last words were something about " lofting down on to a slope with a mashie."

His hole—two down.

### XII.—ST. THOMAS. 450 YARDS.

A driving hole in which you must keep straight. A slice lands in a field out of bounds, or on whins or rough ground ; a pull, into the sea or on to a sharp slope. Whin hazards on both sides for the approach, a hollow and a ridge intervening.

The Professor went down the slope on the left. He smilingly informed me that he always did, and on the whole preferred it, as he thereby got a longer ball. I had a long and straight one. He certainly put a pretty brassie shot on the ridge between the whin hazards, and I was only a little better.

The distance to the green on a slope towards the sea seemed an easy iron shot. The Professor took his brassie and went beyond; I took my iron and lay short. Then I knew how much easier it is to putt uphill than down, for he did the hole in six and I took seven. Of course local knowledge is everything, and I lost this hole because I did not know the green. I admit the Professor explained, but again I did not listen.

Three down !

## XIII.—RABBIT HOLE.   260 YARDS.

He has a stroke here, and from the place where his ball has pitched from the tee he will want it. He sliced it away behind a ridge. I must be careful, for there is a whinney gully in front, and a sandy rabbit bunker to the right. By the guiding flag there is a level piece of good grass, on which I placed my ball. The Professor's brassie shot did *not* land him on the green, as he explained to me it once had; mine did, and I won. This is a pretty green, in a cup and on a slope full of hazards, and with wonderful turf considering its position.

Two down.

## XIV.—MARSH HOLE.   300 YARDS.

This is one of the prettiest holes I have ever played. A fair drive over abundant hazards gives you a good lie, on which a perfect brassie shot lands you on the green. A very fine drive provides a lie from which an iron shot reaches the green. Anything other than fair or fine is useless, or worse. A superb drive may get close to the green, but has to cross awful hazards, the landing in any one of which is ruin. Whin, marsh, sand bunker, stone wall, are amongst the hazards, and all must be avoided.

Well, I was on the green in two perfect shots, and he wasn't ; in fact he played his sixth out of a sand bunker, so I won.

One down.

### XV.—BLOW HOLE. 290 YARDS.

An uphill hole, with an excellent green, protected by a sand bunker. Good drives for good lies, no particular hazard save the sand bunker for the green.

16

Two fine drives, and I must admit the
Professor overdrove me.   He has a stroke here,
and he clearly meant to win.   For once, he
gave me no advice.   I did not want it, for I
saw the flag a full iron shot off.   I forgot
that it was uphill, and got into the bunker.
He took his brassie—he is very fond of his
brassie—and got to the right of the green.
With bad luck in my putt, I halved the hole.
But he had a stroke here, and won.

Two down and three to play.   This looks
bad ; I must play up.

### XVI.—CAMP.   260 YARDS.

Drive over a wall ; a beautiful green, protected by sand bunkers and rough ridges.

Here the Professor foozled his drive and got
under the wall, where I had the satisfaction
of seeing him play back and get over in three.

His fourth shot, not a bad one, landed him in the sand bunker, and he holed out seven to my four.

One down and two to play.

## XVII.—WORLE. 220 YARDS.

I hit the direction-post, or nearly did so, with a grand drive ; the Professor fouled, but put in a decent second, which he said was on the green. It was, as I found when I got up to play my second. That bad drive of the Professor was not properly punished. I got inside him with a cut mashie approach, but there was nothing in it. It is a lovely green, and I holed out in my third with a perfect putt. He tried for a gobble, failed, and went well down the hill. My hole, in spite of the stroke.

All square, and one to play. This is exciting !

## XVIII.—HOME. 350 YARDS.

A driving hole, with driving hazards of roads and rabbit-holes to the left. A lovely flat green, with slope on the left and ridge in front.

Here the Professor took off his coat and gave it to his caddie. He tightened up the vermilion belt which he wears to keep his back steady and save his rheumatic loins, and he repeatedly breathed, I will not say spat, on his palms.

" You see the flag and you see the hazards," he said, and nothing more. I sent off a fair ball. He went up to his ball with his teeth clenched and his eyes fixed and glaring, and he sent it flying in a way I have never seen the Professor do before. For his second, he handled three clubs and fixed on an old and half-cracked driver. He positively put the ball

on the green. So did I. He was ten feet
from the hole. I was twenty. He holed out;
I didn't, but I lipped the hole and was dead.
Of course I cannot guarantee against flukes,
and a ten-feet putt is a fluke, even if the green
be as perfect as was this one.

And so I was beaten. By a fluke certainly,
but by very fine play before the fluke. The
Professor himself admitted that he had never
played such a game in his life before; I
believed him.

Then we had lunch at the fine old Woodspring Priory, and in the afternoon a foursome,
in which the Professor and I were partners.
Herein the Professor did not distinguish himself,
but—we won, and I need not give particulars.

Then tea; then dinner; then the Club wines
and liqueurs; then the Club music, which I
shall not soon forget; then dreams of Woodspring and the Bay and the Ben Barrow holes,

with a confused intermingling of the Nine
Muses of Golf and the Eight Canons of
Woodspring Priory ; and next morning, standing
out through it all, a vivid recollection of a
marvellous bowl of whisky toddy brewed by
the Professor, in the consumption of which he
challenged me to a match and "downed" me.

# Woodspring Priory.

# Woodspring Priory.

BY ONE OF OUR VISITORS.

HE grey walls and tower of the church of Woodspring, with the remains of the conventual buildings, set down at the foot of the sunny slope of the Swallow-cliff, compose a picture of quiet beauty, rarely to be equalled, more rarely excelled.

The Priory, though not remote, has no near neighbours; it has the right feeling of seclusion, without being shut in. As Charles II. said of Godolphin, that he was never in the way, and yet never out of the way, so we may say of Woodspring, that it is not in the world, and yet not out of the world; so far, indeed, is it from

17

129

being shut in, that a description of the views
from the headland behind would be a catalogue
of the hills and dales that border the Severn
Sea.  On days, and those not few, the eye may
wander from the Cotswolds to the Mendips, by
the Quantocks to Exmoor, over the Channel to
Gower, then to the Brecknock Beacons, the
Sugar Loaf at Abergavenny, and the Malvern
Hills.  There is not only distance, but distinction ; as to colour, the miraculous variety of the
colour on the Severn sea and its shore is almost
a commonplace.

To make those who know not the place feel
the subtle charm of it would need the pen of a
Pater : to him it would have appealed strongly,
and there is no one who could analyse the
feelings the place excites more acutely, or
suggest and arouse them more vividly.  It is
not merely that restfulness and a quiet content
pervade the place, not merely that it is perfectly

adapted to the purpose to which it was devoted,
but that the spirit of mediævalism, strong
though elusive, enters into and remains in the
Priory and its precincts as it does in few places.
Walter Pater could have told one how and why
it so does; the cause is in part, but not entirely,
the absence of distracting and ill-accordant
sights and sounds: the happy sounds that greet
the ear are, the clamour of the jackdaws in the
tower, the cawing of the rooks in the elms round
the old fishponds [now dried up], and, more
faintly, the lapping of the waves and plaintive
cries of the sea birds over the hill. Were there
no other inducement to walk round the headland, the feel of the turf would constrain one
to it.

The place is saturated with sunlight and
sweet air; not only is one conscious of life, but
is clothed with it as with a garment, a garment
the feel of which is that of the water in a

moorland stream below a fall on a fair summer day.

Woodspring [or Worspring[1] as it was called aforetime] is in the parish of Kewstoke, in the hundred of Winterstoke; which place, according to Collinson, had its name from the ancient but now depopulated village of Winterstoke, near Banwell. This hundred contains twenty-seven parishes, including most of the Mendip Hills.

The Manor of Woodspring belonged, in the time of Edward the Confessor, to Euroacer, of whom nothing appears to be known save that he owned several manors in the county,[2] and was the father of a son, Aelfric, who, at the time of Domesday Survey, held an estate at Brent Marsh, under Glastonbury Abbey. At

[1] The earliest date at which the name Woodspring appears is, to my knowledge, 1637, in the map of Somerset in Philemon Holland's translation of Camden's *Britannia*.

[2] The positive philologist of tender years would say this was a mythical name, meaning no more than "the man of broad acres."

the Conquest this manor, with some fourteen others, or parts of other manors, was granted to Serlo de Burci; one of his daughters married William de Falaise, bringing Woodspring as her portion. It appears to have descended to Sibil de Falaise, who [in 1102] married Baldwin de Bollers. After the extinction of the male line of de Bollers it passed to the heirs of Sibil; viz., Robert de Courtenay, William de Courtenay, Richard Engaine, and William de Cantelupe; a partition was evidently made, some one or more taking Worle, another or others Kewstoke, whilst Woodspring fell to William de Courtenay.

The value of the manor was assessed in Domesday Book at £4, and its area 7½ hides and 3 fertines, roughly about 2,370 acres. The actual acreage was, however, in all probability much greater, as marsh lands were unmeasured and unassessed.

From the fact of Robert de Courtenay
[father of the founder of the Priory] having
been buried at Woodspring, there was, most
probably, a chapel or chantry on the site ; but
no trace of it has been found, except a Norman
capital, which was dug up some years ago, at a
distance of about 300 yards from the present
church. This is now in the wall at the entrance
gate, From a description given by an old
farmer, however, in 1835, there would appear to
have been some slight resemblance to a small
nave and chancel at a spot known as the Five
Elms, where, underneath some stone slabs, a
quantity of bones was discovered. This is all
that is known of the original building.

Dugdale says that there was at Dodelyng, in
the county of Somerset, a house of Canons
Regular, of the rule of St. Austin and the order
of St. Victor, dedicated to the Blessed Virgin
and St. Thomas à Becket. No such place as

Dodelyng is now known; this house is stated to have been founded by Geoffrey Gilberyn, a benefactor to Woodspring. The community was removed to Woodspring by William de Courtenay in 1210, and a priory founded by him and dedicated to the Holy Trinity, St. Mary the Virgin, and St. Thomas the Martyr.

William de Courtenay appears to have been descended from one or other of the assassins of St. Thomas à Becket, and it is assumed, with some probability, that the Priory owes its foundation to a desire on his part to expiate his ancestor's crime. It is to be remarked, however, that à Becket was murdered in 1170, and William de Courtenay says nothing to show that there was any such desire in his letter to the Bishop of Bath in 1210, announcing his intention to found a conventual house at Woodspring, and asking the Bishop's approval. In this letter (an autograph preserved in the

Cottonian Library) he states that he proposes
founding it for the good of the souls of his
father Robert, there buried, of his mother,
himself, his wife, and those of his ancestors and
descendants; the latter mere general words,
for he had none. There was discovered at
Kewstoke, in about 1849, a reliquary containing
some coagulated blood; the relic is, with great
probability, presumed to have come from Woodspring, and the blood to be à Becket's; even
if these presumptions were verified it does
not prove the founder's intention, for every
church liked to have some relic of the Saint
to which it is dedicated; the seal, however,
which is described later, supports the tradition.

William de Courtenay gave to the Priory all
his lands at Woodspring, and a fardel [a fourth
part of a yard land = thirty acres] in Northamnies.
Geoffrey Gilbewyn gave the Manor of Locking.
In an inspeximus of a charter of Jocelin, Bishop

of Wells, dated 1216, he confirms the gift to the Canons of Doddelinch by the Lord Wm. de Courtenay of the Church of Worle, and that by Master Geoffrey de Gibwine of the Church of Locking. Hugh de Newton gave two messuages and eighty acres of arable land in Norton, and nine acres of meadow, &c., in Woodspring, with licence to have a free and spacious road along the grounds of the said Hugh towards Wampullesser. In 1226 William de Cantilupe, jun., gave 50s. rent and lands, with belongings, in Wurle; and if the lands did not produce that amount, William, sen., agreed to make it up. We do not know when the various buildings were erected, but it would almost seem from the various gifts noted below that special efforts were being made in about 1266 and 1380 to clear the Priory from debt, incurred probably by building.

A number of gifts are referred to and con-

firmed in a charter dated 132$\frac{4}{8}$ [18 Ed. II.],
and stated to have been made to John (Prior
in 1266), viz.: Henry and John Engayne gave
the Manor of Worle, and various homages
and services. Robert Offre, or de Ouvre, gave
six acres of arable and one of meadow, and
Maud his wife all her lands in Chandfeld,
and several parcels of land at Sandford, Bick-
noller, and other places. Alice, the daughter
of the said Maud and Robert de Ouvre, con-
firmed her mother's grants, and gave four
acres of arable land in Sulesworth, one acre
in Sulfebrodacre, three acres in le Heye,
half an acre of meadow in, Estredolmore, and
half an acre of meadow in Westredolmore.
John, son of Robert de Eston, gave the homage
of Martin de la Cume in Milton. Henry, the
son of John de Pendency, gave certain messuages and curtilages at Pendeney, and lands
in Locking and Lockingcroft. [This may

refer to the same gift as that described as a messuage and virgate of land in Locking comprised in a fine dated 4 Ed. I. 1275-6, being a gift by Henry de Pendency.] Henry Limeshest gave the service of Robert Wrech for lands in Sandford and Woodborough. Richard de Hordwell gave lands in Locking.

By a charter of John the Prior and the Canons, given in their Chapter at Woodspring, 16th August, A.D. 1266, in return for many benefits received during life from William de Wichamstede, prepositus of Coombe, and Alex de Bamfeld, Canon of Wells, and for a bequest of 100 marcs, they found a chantry of 53s. 4d. in the Cathedral (Wells) on behalf of the souls of their benefactors, &c.; by another charter of the same date they promise to observe the obit in their own house also. By a charter also given in 1266 by John the Prior, &c., to John de Axebrugge, Subdean of Wells, and to the Dean

and Chapter after him, of an annual payment
of 20s. to be expended in masses for the soul
of the said John, in the Cathedral. By
another charter of John the Prior, &c., given
in the Chapter at Woodspring 4th July, A.D.
1277, in consideration of the gifts made by
William de Button, Bishop of Bath and Wells,
the second, and of a legacy of 210 marcs, the
Priory founds a chantry in the Cathedral of
the value of ten marcs yearly. The Bishop's
legacy had come at a time of need, and enabled
the Convent to redeem an annual payment of
£10 due to the Lord John de Engayne, knight,
upon the Manor of Worle.

In 1291 the Prior and Canons entered into
a bond to pay certain sums to the Dean and
Chapter of Wells for the obit of R. Lofuntun,
probably a benefactor.

Some of the payments above mentioned
would appear to have fallen into arrear, for

in a Convocation of the Dean and Chapter of Wells, 26th September, A.D. 1365, it was ordered that the arrears of Woodspring pension be remitted, but that full payment be demanded for the future.

In 1310, John de Cagayn allowed the Prior a rent of 20s.

In 1331, by patent, Henry Cary, Vicar of Locking, gave some Montfort property, a messuage and fifty-eight acres of land, sevenpence rent and a rent of twelve horse-shoes, in Samford-juxta-Churchill.

In 1331, by charter, Thomas the Prior, &c., agreed to pay a corrody of a quarter of wheat, undoubtedly to some benefactor. In the same year also the Dean and Chapter of Wells (notwithstanding the statute to the contrary) granted a "license to Elyas Spelly, Walter Derby, Thomas Beaupyne of Bristol, to grant in *puram elemosynam* to Thomas the Prior of

Worspryng and to his Canons, a messuage,
dovecote and lands which Richard Dacton,
knight, now holds in Wells, and in Hautrych,
in Northcory, of them *in capite*."

In 1410, by patent, Robert Pobelowe, clerk,
and John Venables, gave 174 acres of land in
Worle, Wynescombe, Rolleston, and Poke-
rolleston, and seven acres in Worspring, the
land of Robert More, the same passing after
his death to the said Robert and John : and
also two acres in Worle, the land of Agnes
Andrew—also destined to pass, after her death,
to the same Robert and John, and so to the
Priory. It appears by an Inquisition *post mortem*,
Henry VII., that 100 acres in Banwell were
held of the Prior and Convent of St. Thomas
Worspring.

Such were the gifts to Woodspring, of which
we have records ; there undoubtedly were in-
numerable others of which we know nothing.

Of the internal history of the Priory, as of its domestic economy, we know but little : there are records of institutions by the Prior and Canons to the livings of Locking, Kewstoke, and Worle ; the discussions as to these and the election of a new Prior seem to have been the greatest causes of excitement to the house, and if lack of history is a true test the community must have been a happy one.

There were the usual services to attend : occasional visits to be made to the granges and distant possessions of the house and to other convents : the home farm and gardens to be looked after, guests to be entertained, the choir to be instructed ; and it is quite probable there was a school for a few boys ; vestments, &c., to be made and repaired ; indeed, a skilful worker would seem to have been in demand, for we read of xii*d.* being paid by the churchwardens of Yatton to a Canon

from Woodspring for repairing vestments.
There was, in all probability, a scriptorium
where the deeds relating to leases, gifts, and
other formal transactions were engrossed, and
possibly books transcribed : if there was no
library, there were almost certainly the usual
books to be found in a convent of the means
of Woodspring : there were the poor of the
neighbourhood to be fed ; at the time of the
Dissolution there was an annual sum of £8
set aside for charitable purposes, being about a
tithe of the income of the house.

In 1309, it is recorded that the Bishop remitted a fine of 20s. due for the non-dedication
of the church and high altar : this would seem
to show, either that they had been desecrated
by some means, or rebuilt for some reason :
this may have been the occasion when the
tower was rebuilt.

In October, 1317, Brother Thomas le Taverner,

of Woodspring, was convicted of rebellion against rule, and confessed. The Bishop decreed that he should be confined in the Priory until the brethren were convinced of his penitence; he was then to take the lowest place, and severe rules of fasting, devotions, silence, and scourging were imposed on him; and anyone neglecting these injunctions was to be excommunicated. He would seem to have been impenitent, or for some other reason was transferred to Bruton Priory, to be kept until penitent under similar conditions, at the cost of his own house.

A like decree was passed upon Canon Lundrais, about the same time, directed to the Prior of Woodspring.

In 1419 the Prior was summoned for causing obstruction by placing bars on the wall called Wowall, the said wall being a common way.

The next notice of the Priory foreshadows the end. A letter, dated early in 1534, records

19

that the writer was "enformed by one of my lordes tenauntes that the Prior of Wulspring shall be deposed shortly."

On the 21st August, 1534, the Priors and Canons surrendered and signed their acknowledgment that the Bishop of Rome was usurper, and that King Henry was alone the Supreme Head of the Church of England.

This document itself is in the Augmentation Office, and is in excellent condition ; the seal, which is of red wax, represents an ancient church over an arch, underneath which is the head, undoubtedly of St. Thomas à Becket, wearing a mitre. There is a hand holding the hilt of a sword with a recurved cross-guard, and a blade cutting down into the front horn of the mitre. There is also a hand, with a cuff like the apparel of an alb, coming out from the dexter side of the arch over the chalice, and appearing to grasp it. A stroke or

line—undecipherable, extends from this hand
to the altar below. The inscription reads :
" Sig + Sancti + Thome De Worspring."

The dissolution was under the Statute 27
Henry VIII. cap 28 [4th February, 1536],
by which **every** religious house, whose income
was less than £200 per annum, was given to
**the** Crown. Woodspring being assessed **at**
£87 2s. 11½d., fell under this **Act.**

The Prior and Canons were driven **out in**
September, 1534, notwithstanding their attempt
to stave off destruction by granting **a farm to**
Sir John Seyntlow, a man of great influence in
the neighbourhood : the Prior **was granted** a
pension of £12 per **annum, and the Sub-Prior**
and Canons [then apparently **only five in**
number] some pittance. In **1553 there remained**
chargeable in fees to members of **this** house the
sum of £1 6s. 8d. There **seem never** to have
been more than ten **Canons,** though of course

there would have been some lay brothers and servants.

The Priors appear to have been :

Reginald, upon whose death Richard, Canon of Keynsham, was elected on Tuesday next after the Assumption, A.D. 1243.

John was Prior in 1266—1277; but the dates of his election and death are not known.

Reginald was Prior in 1317, when he purchased forty acres of land in Woodborough of Henry Loveshate for the use of the Convent.

Thomas was Prior in 1383.

Thomas de Banwell, Prior, died in 1414.

Peter Lobiwra [or Loviare] elected the same year.

William Lusche [or Lustre] died in 1457.

John Gurman [or Turman] elected in 1458.

Richard Spring was Prior in 1498, and resigned in 1525; and the last Prior was Roger Tormenton.

A remarkable letter, dated 9th April, 1536, from Sir Humphrey Stafford to Cromwell, is preserved: in this Sir H. Stafford asked for the Priory to be granted to him; but the extensive manors, &c., were granted to Sir Wm. St. Loe, who, in the 8th Elizabeth, sold that of Woodspring to William Carre,[1] merchant, alderman and M.P. for Bristol; from him it descended by a collateral heiress to William Yonge, of Ogborne St. George, and now belongs to the trustees of the late Cecil Smith Pigott, Esq., of Brockley Hall.

A church itself being actually converted into a domestic establishment is extremely rare; but such is the case at Woodspring, the whole of the nave and the north aisle forming part of the

[1] From the inquisition taken the 7th April, 1579, on his death, the reversion in fee appears to have descended to his eldest son and heir, John Carr, expectant on estates tail in his brother Edward and others; this reversion was released to Edward Carr in 1589.

farm-house.[1]   It remains to describe briefly the buildings as they now stand.

On each side of the roadway near the entrance gateway are two projections ornamented with escutcheons, on one of which is blazoned the five stigmata or wounds of our Saviour; on the other, a chevron between three bugles ; the projections are probably modern, the escutcheons from the old buildings.

The entrance consists of a large gateway, with a smaller door on the north side. The arches in both cases are segmental, a form not uncommon in buildings of the 14th century. The gateway opens into a court or garth, bounded on the north by a range of domestic

[1] It is believed that Woodspring was, from about 1600 to 1725, used as a hospital for "poor and maimed soldiers," as there are between those dates frequent entries in the overseers' account books of adjacent parishes of contributions made towards a hospital for that purpose: Woodspring itself appears only to be named in Kewstoke entries for 1722 and 1725; but there is little doubt that the other references are also to it.

buildings, probably of Post-reformation date, though some parts, particularly the string course, may be older; and on the west by the wall of the cloisters, which retains some fine gurgoyles. Immediately in front of the gateway is the west front of the church, mutilated by the insertion of modern windows. The large west window, now built up, occupied nearly the whole of this front, rising from a bold string course, which extends from buttress to buttress: these are in the form of octagonal turrets. The cornice moulding of the building passes round these turrets, which are raised above it, and terminate with an embattled parapet, under which is a course of quatrefoils, each side of the octagon being occupied by one quatrefoil within a square. On each side of the window was a canopied niche, and there appears to have been a similar one above: this, and that on the south, have been totally obliterated; in that on the

north an episcopal figure may still be traced. On
the south side of the tower is a staircase turret,
terminating in a pyramidal pinnacle, with a
finial and parapet of Tudor flowers, an arrangement very common in this neighbourhood. On
the north side is an aisle of three bays (having
an entrance to the church in that at the western
extremity), extending as far as the eastern side
of the tower, into which it opened by a splendid
arch. The chancel or choir, which, as in all
conventual buildings, was long, no doubt ex-
tended much to the east of the tower, and took
away from the apparent height of the church.
It is now totally destroyed, though the chancel
arch remains.

A writer in the *Antiquary* for 1881 says :
" The tower in the 13th century was probably
low and squat, and certainly massive, with
scanty elevation for bells; and its summit was
reached by an external stair flight. It stands

now in a 15th century case, and is topped by an
upper stage of the same date; whilst again its
lower story contains an inner skin of light
Perpendicular work in whitish Caen stone, with
open arches elegantly supported on recessed
shafts, and a fan vaulting springing from each
angle. It is not often that we meet so curious
a piece of incrustation of style by style in such
thorough harmony of spirit, yet such startling
contrast of form.

"The later casing, however, is not symmetrical
with the proportions of the original tower, the
ground plan of which was not square but
oblong, whilst that of the later tower distributed
its enlarged sides unequally between the north
and south sides. On both these sides the older
tower, or what was left of it by the 15th
century architect, stands masked under a stone
pent-house with sloping roof, having something
of the air of a buttress broadened out; but in

20

the north side the front of the ground plan was
advanced to take in the projection of the
external flight of stairs above referred to, which
the later south face conceals, all save the upper
portion. These stairs only rise to about one-
third of the height of the later and taller tower,
which would be about one-half of the height of
the older and shorter one. This width, on what
we may call the first floor of his tower, the later
architect has turned to account by creating a
little parapet walk of a few paces between the
southern wall face of his own tower and the
casing of the old. . . . The internal corbels
in the second story of the tower entered from
the stairs are part of the old structure, and mark
something [probably the framework on which
the bells were hung] which disappeared when it
was altered. . . . The tower once terminated
in a pinnacle at each angle, with an added
secondary in the middle of each of its faces."

The parapet is worked in a continuous series of framed panels, every panel having an open quatrefoil set in a square, and every quatrefoil an ornament of fruit or foliage, all worked with as loving and artistic care as if intended to be seen on the level of the ground.

The remains of the cloisters, which are of the 14th century, occupy the space on the south of the nave and tower, the west wall of the enclosure standing flush with the west front of the church; the pitch of the cloister roof is distinctly marked upon the wall over the door into the farmhouse. All vestiges of the interior of these cloisters have vanished, with the exception of what appears to be a corbel table and the entrance to a small turret at the south-west corner. Opposite to this there was a passage to the refectory; and on the east wall of the enclosure are two arches, now built up, and the mutilated remains of a doorway, the arch of

which is of the Decorated character, and must,
with its elaborated cusps, have been exceedingly
beautiful. The domestic buildings of the Priory,
including the Prior's lodging, occupied the
greater part of the orchard on the east of the
church, as is evident from the marks of founda-
tions extending nearly over its whole extent.
All these, however, are gone, with the exception
of the refectory, now used as a waggon-house.
This is a beautifully-proportioned room of Early
Perpendicular character, 45 feet long and 19
wide; the eastern part has suffered from time
and ill-usage, but the rest is nearly perfect. On
the north side it was lighted by two windows,
traces of which still remain; they are of two
lights, and divided by a transom. Two door-
ways give access to this fine hall: one at the
west end, over which is a small window of two
lights; the other at the east end of the north
side, the very elaborate mouldings of which are

still in fine preservation. A staircase turret, in
ruins, is on the south side, but there seem no
traces of a fireplace.

Time has but added to the glory of the
monastic barn, which stands in a perfect state
on the north side of the Priory; and these
much despoiled but beautiful fragments are all
that remain of the magnificent foundation of
William de Courteney.

# farewell.

STILL week by week we go the same old round ;
   Still we can drive Ben Barrow and the Bay ;
   And sometimes still our best shots go astray
At Middle Hope, St. Thomas, or the Pound.
Still we can top, and slice, and take the ground,
   And still deplore each other's style of play ;
   Still Fido goes his melancholy way,
And in our book no minutes can be found.

All is the same ; but now we may not meet
   One comrade who was here with us before.
Made is the record he had hoped to beat,
   Played his last stroke, and added up his score.
Lost is one note, our "octave" incomplete,
   The voice we listen for is heard no more !

www.ingramcontent.com/pod-product-compliance
Lightning Source LLC
Chambersburg PA
CBHW021109020726
47500CB00003B/679